CHILDREN'S
STORYTIME COLLECTION

Buried Treasure

AND OTHER STORIES

Contents

The Castle in the Clouds

There was once a family that lived in a little house in a village at the bottom of a mountain. At the top of the mountain was a great, grey castle made of granite. The castle was always shrouded in clouds, so it was known as the castle in the clouds. From the village you could only just see the outline of its high walls and turrets. No-one in the village ever went near the castle, for it looked such a gloomy and forbidding place.

Now in this family there were seven children. One by one they went out into the world to seek their fortune, and at last it was the youngest child's turn. His name was Sam. His only possession was a pet cat named Jess, and she was an excellent rat-catcher. Sam was most upset at the thought of leaving Jess behind when he went off to find work, but then he had an idea.

"I'll offer Jess's services at the castle in the clouds. They're bound to need a good ratter, and I'm sure I can find work there, too," he thought.

His parents were dismayed to discover that Sam intended to seek work at the castle, but try as they might they could not change his mind. So Sam set off for the castle with Jess at his side. Soon the road started to wind up the mountainside through thick pine forests. It grew cold and misty. Rounding a bend they suddenly found themselves up against a massive, grey stone wall. They followed the curve of the wall until they came to the castle door.

Sam went up to the door and banged on it. The sound echoed spookily. "Who goes there?" said a voice.

Looking up, Sam saw that a window high in the wall had been thrown open and a face was eyeing him suspiciously.

3

"I… I… I wondered if you'd be interested in employing my cat as a rat-catcher," began Sam.

The window slammed shut, but a moment later a hand beckoned him through the partly open castle door. Stepping inside, Sam and Jess found themselves face-to-face with an old man. "Rat-catcher, did you say?" said the old man raising one eyebrow. "Very well, but she'd better do a good job or my master will punish us all!"

Sam sent Jess off to prove her worth. In the meantime Sam asked the old man, who was the castle guard, if there might be any work for him, too.

"You can help out in the kitchens. It's hard work, mind!" the guard said.

Sam was soon at work in the kitchens – and what hard work it was! He spent all day peeling vegetables, cleaning pans and scrubbing the floor. By midnight he was exhausted. He was about to find a patch of straw to make his bed, when he noticed Jess wasn't around. He set off in search of her. Down dark passages he went, up winding staircases, looking in every corner and behind every door, but there was no sign of her. By now he was hopelessly lost and was wondering how he would ever find his way back to the kitchens, when he caught sight of Jess's green eyes shining like lanterns at the top of a rickety spiral staircase. "Here, Jess!" called Sam softly. But Jess stayed just where she was.

When he reached her, he found that she was sitting outside a door and seemed to be listening to something on the other side. Sam put his ear to the door. He could hear the sound of sobbing. He knocked gently at the door. "Who is it?" said a girl's voice.

"I'm Sam, the kitchen boy. What's the matter? Can I come in?" said Sam.

"If only you could," sobbed the voice. "I'm Princess Rose. When my father died my uncle locked me in here so that he could steal the castle. Now I fear I shall never escape!"

Sam pushed and pushed at the door, but to no avail. "Don't worry," he said, "I'll get you out of here."

Sam knew exactly what to do, for when he had been talking to the guard, he had spotted a pair of keys hanging on a nail in the rafters high above the old man's head. He had wondered at the time why anyone should put keys out of the reach of any human hand. Now he thought he knew – but first he had to get the keys himself!

Sam and Jess finally made their way back to where the keys were, only to find the guard was fast asleep in his chair right underneath them! Quick as a flash, Jess had leaped up on to the shelf behind his head. From there, she climbed higher and higher until she reached the rafters. She took the keys in her jaws and carried them gingerly down. But as she jumped from the shelf again, she knocked over a jug and sent it crashing to the floor. The guard woke with a start. "Who goes there?" he growled. He just caught sight of the tip of Jess's tail as she made a dash for the door.

Sam and Jess retraced their steps with the guard in hot pursuit. "You go a different way," hissed Sam, running up the stairs to Rose's door, while the old man disappeared off after Jess. Sam put one of the keys in the lock. It fitted! He turned the key and opened the door. There stood the loveliest girl he had ever seen. The princess ran towards him, as he cried, "Quick!

There's not a moment to lose." He grabbed her hand
and led her out of the tower.

"Give me the keys," she said. She led him down to the
castle cellars. At last they came to a tiny door. The
princess put the second key in the lock and the
door opened. Inside was a small cupboard, and
inside that was a golden casket filled with precious
jewels. "My own casket – stolen by my uncle," cried Rose.

Grabbing the casket the pair ran to the stables and saddled a
horse. Suddenly Jess appeared with the guard still chasing him.
With a mighty leap Jess landed on the back of the horse behind
the princess and Sam. "Off we go!" cried Sam.

And that was the last that any of them saw of the castle in
the clouds. Sam married the princess and they all lived happily
ever after.

Buried Treasure

Jim lived in a big old house with a big rambling garden. The
house was rather spooky, and Jim much preferred the garden. He
would spend hours kicking a football around the overgrown lawn,
climbing the old apple trees in the orchard or just staring into the
pond in case he might spot a fish. It was a wonderful garden to
play in but Jim was not really a happy child because he was
lonely. How he wished he had someone to play with! It would be
such fun to play football with a friend, or have someone to go
fishing with. He had plenty of friends at school, but it was a long
bus journey to his home and besides, his school friends found his
house so spooky that they only came to visit once.

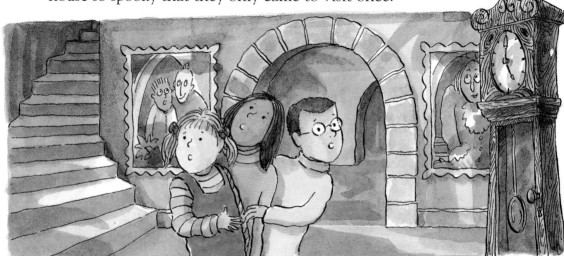

One day Jim was hunting about in the garden with a stick. He hoped he might find some interesting small creatures to examine. Every time he found a new creature he would draw it and try to find out its name. So far, he had discovered eight types of snails and six different ladybirds. As he was poking about under some leaves he saw a piece of metal sticking out of the ground. He reached down and pulled it free. In his hand lay a rusty old key. It was quite big, and as Jim brushed away the soil, he saw that it was carved with beautiful patterns.

Jim carried the key indoors and cleaned it and polished it. Then he set about trying to find the lock that it fitted. First he tried the old garden gate that had been locked as long as Jim could remember. But the key was far too small. Next he tried the grandfather clock in the hall. But the key did not fit the clock's lock. Then he remembered an old wind-up teddy bear that played the drum. Jim hadn't played with the toy for a long time and he eagerly tried out the key, but this time it was too big.

Then Jim had another idea. "Perhaps the key fits something in the attic," he thought. He was usually too scared to go into the attic on his own because it really was scary. But now he was so determined to find the key's home that he ran up the stairs boldly and opened the door. The attic was dimly lit, dusty and full of cobwebs. The water pipes hissed and creaked and Jim shivered. He began to look under a few dustsheets and opened some old boxes, but didn't find anything that looked like it needed a key to unlock it. Then he caught sight of a large book sticking out from one of the shelves. It was one of those sorts of books fitted with a lock. Jim lifted down the book, which was extremely heavy, and put it on the floor. His fingers trembled as he put the key in the lock. It fitted perfectly. He turned the key and the lock sprang open, releasing a cloud of dust. Jim wiped the dust from his eyes, slowly opened the book and turned the pages.

What a disappointment! The pages were crammed with tiny
writing and there were no pictures at all. Jim was about to shut
the book again when he heard a voice. The voice was coming
from the book! "You have unlocked my secrets," it said. "Step
into my pages if you are looking for adventure."

Jim was so curious that he found himself stepping on to the
book. As soon as he put his foot on the pages he found himself
falling through the book. The next thing he knew he was on the
deck of a ship. He looked up and saw a tattered black flag flying
from a flagpole and on the flag were a skull and crossbones. He
was on a pirate ship! He looked down and saw that he was
dressed like a pirate.

The pirate ship was sailing along nicely, when suddenly Jim
saw some dangerous-looking rocks in the water – and they were
heading straight for them! Before he could shout, the ship had
run aground and all the pirates were jumping overboard and
swimming to the shore. Jim swam, too.

The water felt deliciously warm and when he reached the shore he found warm sand between his toes. He couldn't believe it! Here he was on a desert island. The pirates went in all directions, searching for something to make a shelter. Jim looked, too, and under a rock he found a book. The book looked familiar to Jim. He was sure he'd seen it somewhere before. He was still puzzling over it when one of the pirates came running towards him waving a knife. "You thief, you stole me rubies!" cursed the pirate in a menacing voice. What was Jim to do?

Then he heard a voice call out from the book, "Quick! Step into my pages." Without thinking twice, Jim stepped into the book and suddenly he was back in the attic again.

Jim peered closely at the page from which he'd just stepped. *The Pirates and the Stolen Treasure* it said at the top of the page. Jim read the page and found he was reading exactly the adventure he had been in. He turned excitedly to the contents page at the front of the book and read the chapter titles. *Journey to Mars*, he read, and *The Castle Under the Sea*. Further down it said: *The Magic Car* and *Into the Jungle*. Jim was thrilled. He realised that he could open the book at any page and become part of the adventure, and he only had to find the book and step into it to get back to the attic again.

After that, Jim had many, many adventures. He made lots of friends in the stories and he had lots of narrow escapes. But he always found the book again just in time. Jim was never lonely again.

The Very Big Parcel

Once upon a time there lived an old man and his wife. They dwelled in a small house with a small, neat garden and they were very contented. What's more, they had very good friends and neighbours, with whom they shared everything. One day, there was a knock at the door and there stood the postman with a huge parcel in his arms.

"My, oh my!" exclaimed the old man to his wife as he staggered into the kitchen with the enormous load.

"Whatever can it be?" wondered the old woman as the two of them stared at the parcel. "Perhaps it's a new set of china," said she.

"Or a new wheelbarrow," said he. And they began to think about all the fancy things there might be inside the parcel.

"Well, why don't we open it and see?" said the old lady at last. And so they did. They looked into the box and at first it seemed to be totally empty.

"Well, I never did!" cried the old man. And then he spotted something right in the corner of the box. He lifted it out into the light to examine it more carefully and discovered it was a single seed.

Well, the old man and his wife were most upset. Whereas before they were quite content, now that they had thought about all the things that might have been in the box they were bitterly disappointed by the seed. "Still," said the old man at last, "we'd better plant it anyway. Who knows, maybe we'll get a nice fresh lettuce from it."

So he planted the seed in the garden. Every day he watered the ground and soon a shoot appeared. The shoot grew into a strong young plant and then it grew taller and taller. Higher and higher it grew until it was a handsome tree. The man and his wife were excited to see fruits growing on the tree. "I wonder if they're apples," the old man said. Each day he watered the tree and examined the fruits. One day he said to his wife, "The first fruit is ready to pick." He carefully reached up into the tree and picked the large red fruit.

He carried it into the kitchen and put it on the table. Then he took a knife and cut the fruit in half. To his astonishment out poured a pile of gold coins. "Come quickly!" he called to his wife. Well, the pair of them danced round the kitchen for joy.

The old couple decided to spend just one gold coin and keep the rest. "After all," said the woman wisely, "we don't know what's in the other fruits. They may be full of worms." So they spent one golden penny in the town and put the rest aside.

The next day the old man picked another big red fruit and this, too, was full of gold. After that the old couple were less careful with their money, thinking all the fruits must be full of gold.

They had a wonderful time buying fine clothes and things for the house and garden. Each day the man picked another fruit. Each day it was full of gold and each day they went into town and had a grand time spending the money. But all the while the man forgot entirely to water the tree.

Meanwhile, the old couple's friends and neighbours started to gossip among themselves. They wondered where all the money was coming from and they began to resent the old couple. They noticed that the old couple didn't buy anything for their friends, or even throw a party. Gradually their friends ignored them until the old couple were left with no friends at all. But they didn't even notice because they were so busy spending the gold coins.

Then one day the old man looked out into the garden and saw that the tree was all withered. He rushed outside and threw bucket after bucket of water over the tree, but all to no avail.

17

He and his wife frantically picked the fruits left on the tree, but when they took them indoors they found to their dismay that they were cracked and gnarled. When they broke open the fruits they were full of dust. "If only I had not been so thoughtless and remembered to water the tree!" cried the old man in anguish.

The next day the old couple looked out of the window to find that the tree had vanished. Now what were they to do? They had completely neglected to take care of their garden and now they had nothing to eat. They realised that they would have to sell their riches to buy food. Then they also needed new gardening tools, for theirs had grown rusty with neglect.

As the weeks passed, the old man and his wife gradually sold all the fine things they had bought, just to keep body and soul together. They felt truly miserable and sorry for the way they had treated their neighbours. For now they realised just how lonely they were without their friends. "We have no money now," said the wife one day, "but let's have a party anyway. For friendship is more valuable than any amount of gold coins."

So the old couple invited all their friends and neighbours round and they had a grand party. The friends wondered what had happened to all the old couple's riches and what had happened to make the old couple so friendly once more, but I don't think they ever found out, do you?

19

The Invisible Imp

One day, Sarah Jones was pegging out her washing. It was a lovely day and she was looking forward to visiting her friend Rose. "I'll just get this washing on the line while the sun's shining," she said to herself, "and then I'll be on my way."

After a while, she stopped and looked down into the basket. "That's very peculiar!" she thought. "I know I've already pegged out that green shirt and there it is back in the basket." She carried on pegging out the clothes. Now she shook her head in disbelief. For although she had been working away for quite a while, the basket of washing was still full and there was almost nothing on the line! She began to get quite cross, for she was going to be late getting to Rose's house.

Try as she might, she just could not get that washing pegged. In the end, she had to leave the basket of wet washing and run to Rose's house.

"I'm so sorry I'm late, Rose," she gasped, all out of breath from running. Sarah told Rose all about what had happened.

"Well," said Rose, "that's a strange coincidence. I was baking some cakes for us to have for tea. Every time I put them in the oven and turned away, they were out of the oven and on the table again! In the end I had to stand guard over them – which reminds me, they were just beginning to cook nicely when you knocked on the door."

The two women went into Rose's kitchen and there were the cakes, sitting on the table again, half-cooked. "Now they're ruined!" cried Rose. "Whatever shall we do?"

At that moment, there was a noise in the street. Rose and Sarah looked out of the window to see Elmer, the postman, surrounded by a crowd of people all shouting and waving envelopes in the air. The two women ran out into the street. "What's going on?" they cried.

"Elmer's given us all the wrong post," said Rose's neighbour, Dora. "He's normally so reliable, but this morning he seems to have gone completely crazy. Now we've got to sort out all the mail for him."

"I don't know what's happened," wailed Elmer in anguish. "I'm sure I posted all the letters through the right doors."

"Well," said Sarah, "Rose and I have also found strange things happening to us this morning." She told the crowd their stories. Everyone forgave Elmer when they realised it wasn't his fault, but they were still truly mystified as to what – or who – could have caused all these problems.

But that wasn't the end of it. Oh no, indeed! The butcher's wife served her family mutton stew, but when she lifted the lid the family heard a bleating sound and a little lamb leaped out of the pot. The milkman delivered the milk as usual, but when people took their milk indoors, they found the bottles were full of lemonade. Old Mr Smith tried to pull his chair up to the table and found it was stuck hard to the floor. And when Mrs Smith painted her bedroom blue, she came back and found it had changed to pink with purple spots.

Can you guess what had happened? Do you know who'd been up to all these tricks? It was an imp, of course! The wicked little fellow had become bored playing pranks on the fairies and goblins in fairyland. By now, they knew all his tricks and he was finding it harder and harder to catch them out. Then he had an idea. Why not play tricks in the human world where he would be invisible? So that's exactly what he did.

At first, he really only meant
to play one or two tricks, but he
had such fun that he couldn't
resist carrying on.

Well, the invisible imp continued
on with his tricks. But of course, as you know,
pride comes before a fall, and one day he just went too far. Sarah
Jones had been invited to a party. It was to be a fancy dress party
and on the invitation it said: "*Please wear red*". Now Sarah
fretted because she had no red clothes at all. Then she
had an idea. She got out an old blue frock from the
back of the cupboard. "I'll dye it red," she thought.

She mixed a big tub of red dye and was just about to put the
dress into it, when along came the invisible imp. "Here's some
fun!" he thought. "I'll turn the dye blue. Then she won't know
why her dress hasn't changed colour. Won't that be funny!" And
he started giggling to himself at the thought of it. He danced up
and down on the edge of the tub, thinking up
a really evil spell to turn the dye blue.

But he laughed so much to himself
that he slipped and fell right into
the bright red mixture. Fast as
lightning out he scrambled
and cast his spell.

24

Sure enough Sarah fished out the dress from the tub, and to her dismay saw that it was exactly the same colour as when she had put it into the dye. She was about to peer into the tub when something caught her eye. For there, sitting on the table, chuckling to himself and holding his sides with laughter, was a bright red imp. And there was a trail of tiny red footprints from the tub of dye to the table. The silly imp had no idea that he was no longer invisible and that Sarah could see him as plain as the nose on her face! In a flash Sarah realised what had happened. She chased the imp out of the house and down the street and, I'm glad to say, he wasn't able to play his mischievous tricks ever again.

Peter Meets a Dragon

Once upon a time there was a young boy named Peter. He lived in an ordinary house with an ordinary Mum and Dad, an ordinary sister and an ordinary pet cat, called Jasper. In fact, everything in Peter's life was so ordinary that he sometimes wished that something extraordinary would happen. "Why doesn't a giant come and squash the house flat with his foot?" he wondered, and "If only a pirate would take my sister hostage!" But each day, Peter would wake up in the morning and everything was just the same as it had been the day before.

One morning Peter woke up to find a very strange smell in the house. Looking out of his bedroom window, he saw that the front lawn was scorched and blackened. There was smoke drifting off the grass and, further away, he could see some bushes ablaze.

Peter rushed downstairs and out of the front door. He ran out of
the garden and down the lane following the trail of smoke and
burning grass. He grew more and more puzzled, however, as there
was no sign of anything that could have caused such a blaze.

Peter was about to run home and tell his Mum and Dad, when
he heard a panting noise coming from the undergrowth. Parting
the bushes gently with his hands he found a young creature. It
had green, scaly skin, a pair of wings and a long snout full of
sharp teeth. Every now and again a little tongue of flame came
from its nostrils, setting the grass around it on fire. "A baby
dragon!" Peter said to himself, in great surprise. Big tears were
rolling out of the dragon's yellow eyes and down its scaly cheeks
as it flapped its wings desperately and tried to take off.

When the dragon saw Peter it stopped flapping its wings.
"Oh, woe is me!" it sobbed. "Where am I?"

"Where do you want to be?" asked Peter,
kneeling down on the scorched ground.

27

"I want to be in Dragonland with my friends," replied the dragon. "We were all flying together, but I just couldn't keep up with them. I got tired and needed a rest. I called to the others but they didn't hear me. Then I just had to stop and get my breath back. Now I don't know where I am, or if I'll ever see my friends again!" And with that the baby dragon started to cry once more.

"I'm sure I can help. I'll get you home," said Peter, though he had no idea how.

"You?" hissed a voice nearby. "How could you possibly help? You're just a boy!" Peter looked round, and to his astonishment found Jasper sitting behind him. "I suppose you're going to wave a magic wand, are you?" continued Jasper. "You need to call in an expert." Then he turned his back on Peter and the baby dragon and started washing his paws.

Peter was astounded. He'd never heard Jasper talking before. He had thought he was just an ordinary pet cat. "W… w… what do you mean?" he stammered.

"Well," said Jasper, glancing over his shoulder at Peter, "I reckon that horse over there could help. Follow me."

So Peter and the baby dragon – whose name was Flame – followed Jasper over to where the horse stood at the edge of a field. Jasper leaped up on to the gate and called to the horse. Then he whispered in the horse's ear. The horse thought for a moment, then whispered back in Jasper's ear. "He says he's got a friend on the other side of the wood who'll help," said Jasper.

"But how?" said Peter, looking perplexed.

"Be patient! Follow me!" said Jasper as he stalked off through the grass. "And tell your friend to stop setting fire to everything!" he added. Peter saw, to his horror, that Flame was indeed blazing a trail through the field.

"I can't help it," cried Flame, about to burst into tears again. "Every time I get out of breath I start to pant, and then I start breathing fire."

"Let me carry you," said Peter. He picked Flame up in his arms and ran after Jasper. The baby dragon felt very strange. His body was all cold and clammy, but his mouth was still breathing hot smoke, which made Peter's eyes water.

He ran through the wood, just keeping Jasper's upright tail in sight. On the other side of the wood was another field, and in the field was a horse. But this was no ordinary horse. Peter stopped dead in his tracks and stared. The horse was pure milky white, and from its head grew a single, long horn. "A unicorn!" breathed Peter.

Jasper was already talking to the unicorn. He beckoned with his paw to Peter. "He'll take your friend home and you can go, too, Peter, but don't be late for tea, or you know what your mother will say." And with that, Jasper was off.

"Climb aboard," said the unicorn gently.

Peter and the little dragon scrambled up on to the unicorn's back. "What an adventure," thought Peter. Up, up, and away they soared through the clouds.

Flame held tightly on to Peter's hand with his clammy paw. At last Peter could see a mountain ahead through the clouds. Now they were descending through the clouds again, and soon the unicorn landed right at the top of the mountain. "I'm home!" squeaked Flame joyously as they landed. Sure enough, several dragons were running over to greet him. They looked quite friendly, but some of them were rather large and one was breathing a great deal of fire.

"Time for me to go," said Peter a little nervously, as Flame jumped off the unicorn's back and flew to the ground. The unicorn took off again and soon they were back in the field once more.

As he slid off the unicorn's back, Peter turned to thank him, but when he looked he saw that it was just an ordinary horse with no trace of a horn at all. Peter walked back home across the field, but there was no sign of burnt grass. He reached his own front lawn, which was also in perfect condition. Peter felt more and more perplexed. "I hope Jasper can explain," he thought, as the cat ran past him and into the house. "Jasper, I took the baby dragon home. What's happened to the burnt grass?" he blurted out. But Jasper said not a word. He ignored Peter and curled up in his basket.

When Peter wasn't looking, however, Jasper gave him a glance that seemed to say, "Well, was that a big enough adventure for you?"

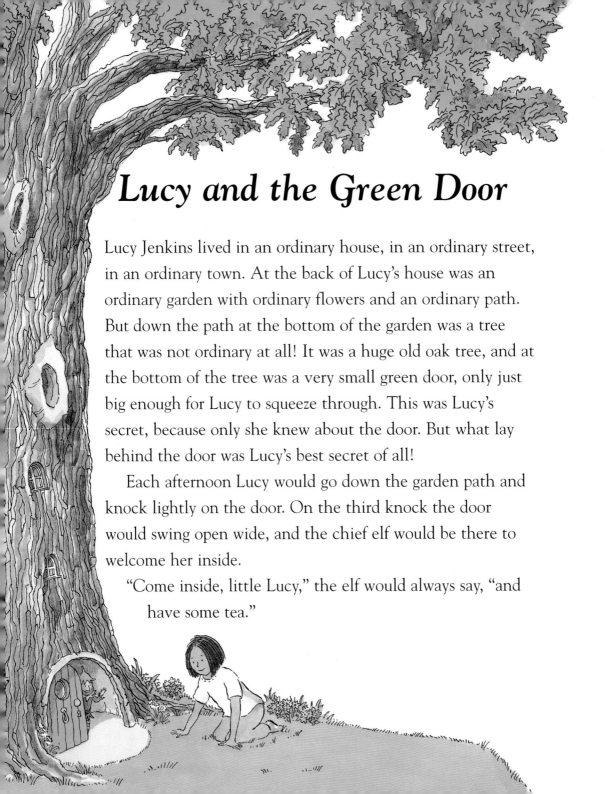

Lucy and the Green Door

Lucy Jenkins lived in an ordinary house, in an ordinary street, in an ordinary town. At the back of Lucy's house was an ordinary garden with ordinary flowers and an ordinary path. But down the path at the bottom of the garden was a tree that was not ordinary at all! It was a huge old oak tree, and at the bottom of the tree was a very small green door, only just big enough for Lucy to squeeze through. This was Lucy's secret, because only she knew about the door. But what lay behind the door was Lucy's best secret of all!

Each afternoon Lucy would go down the garden path and knock lightly on the door. On the third knock the door would swing open wide, and the chief elf would be there to welcome her inside.

"Come inside, little Lucy," the elf would always say, "and have some tea."

Inside, Lucy would meet some very special friends indeed! First there were Penelope and Geraldine, two of the gentlest and sweetest fairies it was possible to imagine. Then there were Basil and Granville, who were rather mischievous imps (but who made Lucy laugh with their tricks and jokes), and there were the storytellers, who would sit for hours with Lucy and tell her the greatest tales from all the corners of the world. And of course there was the chief elf, who would make the most delicious milkshakes and scones with heaps of cream for Lucy to eat.

The world behind the green door was a wonderful place, and Lucy would always go home afterwards feeling very cheerful and jolly. On one particular visit to the world behind the green door Lucy had just finished a scrumptious tea of cocoa and toasted marshmallows with the chief elf, when she went off to play games with Basil and Granville. They were playing blind man's buff, and Lucy roared with laughter as Basil sneaked up on the blindfolded Granville and tickled him in the ribs, making him squeal and beg for the teasing to stop.

33

Now just recently, Lucy had been feeling down in the dumps because very soon she would be going to school and would only be able to visit her friends at weekends. But they assured her that they would never forget her, and that as long as she was always a true friend to them she could visit as often or as little as she liked. This cheered Lucy up considerably, and then they took her to visit the storytellers so that her happiness was complete. Of all the delights behind the green door, the storytellers were Lucy's favourite. They told her stories of how the whales had learned to sing, and of where the stars went when the sun had risen in the sky and they had slipped from view.

Because of the assurances of the fairies, Lucy was not too worried when the day finally came for her to join all the other boys and girls of her age at school. Every day, Lucy would go to school and then afterwards would visit her friends behind the green door. As winter came round and the days grew dark she only visited at weekends, and looked forward to the holidays when she could visit them every day once more.

Meanwhile, at school, Lucy had made friends with a girl called Jessica, and although she told Jessica all about her family and her home, she didn't at first tell her about her extraordinary tree with the little green door and the magic world that lay beyond. Lucy did tell Jessica all the stories that she was told by the storytellers, however, and Jessica grew more and more curious about where she had heard all the wonderful tales. Every day, Jessica would ask more and more questions, and Lucy found it more and more difficult to avoid telling her about her secret. Eventually, Lucy gave in and told Jessica all about her adventures behind the green door.

Jessica scoffed and laughed when Lucy told her about the chief elf, and Basil, Granville, Penelope and Geraldine. She howled with laughter at the thought of the wonderful teas and the stories that followed. Jessica thought that Lucy was making the whole thing up! When Lucy protested, and said it was true, Jessica told her that it simply wasn't possible – that there were no such things as elves and fairies and imps and strange and wonderful worlds behind doors in trees. Lucy was distraught, and decided to take Jessica to the green door.

On the way home Lucy started to worry. What if she really had imagined it all? But if her wonderful friends didn't exist, how could she possibly know them? Jessica walked beside Lucy, still teasing her and laughing about Lucy's 'invisible' friends!

When Lucy and Jessica reached the bottom of the garden, Lucy was about to tap lightly on the green door at the bottom of the oak tree when she suddenly noticed the door had disappeared. She rubbed her eyes and looked again, but it simply wasn't there!

Jessica smirked and laughed at Lucy, calling her silly and babyish to believe in magic and fairy tales, and then ran off back down the road to school. Lucy could not face going back to school that afternoon, and when her mother saw her enter the house she thought she must be ill – she looked so upset! Lucy went to bed early and cried herself to sleep.

And when Lucy slept she started to dream. The chief elf, Basil and Granville, Penelope and Geraldine and the storytellers were all there in the dream. Then Penelope and Geraldine stepped forward and hugged Lucy, and the hug was so real that

Lucy began to hope it wasn't a dream! Then
they all hugged her and asked why she
hadn't been to see them for so long, and
why they had not been able to reach
out to her except now in the deepest
of sleeps. Lucy explained what had happened
on her last visit, and told them all about Jessica, and
then Geraldine spoke. "Little Lucy," she said, "you are special.
You believe in magic and you believe in the little people. And
because you believe, you are able to see us and live among us.
But those who don't believe will always be shut out from our
world. You must keep your belief, little Lucy."

With a huge surge of happiness Lucy woke up, dressed quickly
and ran out of her ordinary house, down the ordinary path in the
ordinary garden up to the extraordinary tree, and was delighted to
see the green door once more! She knocked very lightly and, after
the third tap, the door swung open to reveal the chief elf. "Come
inside, little Lucy," the elf said happily, "and have some tea."

Puss in Boots

Once upon a time in France, there lived a miller who had three sons. When he died, the miller left the mill to his eldest son. To his second son he left a donkey on whose back sacks of flour could be loaded and delivered to customers. But to the youngest son, who was much the most handsome of the three, he left only a large cat, whose job it had been to chase the mice that came at night to make holes in the sacks and steal grain.

The poor youngest brother wondered how on earth he would make his living with only the cat for company. He could see that he would have to go out into the world to seek his fortune. "I shall have to leave you behind, Puss," he said, "for I don't see how I am to look after you."

"What about if I looked after *you?*" replied Puss.

"Whatever do you mean?" said his master.

"I can make your fortune for you," said the cat. "All I need is a good – sized drawstring bag and a pair of really nice boots – for my hind feet."

Well, the lad was mightily puzzled, but he decided it was worth letting the cat try to win his fortune, as he surely had no idea of what to do otherwise. With his brand new boots on his hind paws and his drawstring bag slung over his shoulder, Puss set off with nothing but a handful of corn from the mill.

The first thing he did was go straight to the nearest rabbit warren where he opened the bag, put a little corn into it and laid it open near the rabbit hole. Then Puss laid in wait until dusk, when the rabbits came out of their hole. One rabbit came up, full of curiosity, and hopped into the bag to get the corn. Up sprang Puss and pulled the drawstring tight. Then, instead of taking the rabbit to his master, he set off to the palace, where he announced that he had brought the king a present.

"Your majesty," said Puss, taking a low bow, "I am a messenger from the Marquis of Carabas, your neighbour. He was out hunting today and was lucky enough to catch a fine young rabbit. He begs that you will accept it as a present."

The king was puzzled, because he'd never heard of this Marquis, but he was pleased to have the rabbit. "Tell your master that I am delighted with his kind present," he said.

Day after day, Puss went out hunting in this manner and each time he presented his catch to the king. "Don't forget," he said to his master, "that you're supposed to be a Marquis." The young boy had no idea what the cat was talking about, but he trusted him nevertheless. After a while the cat started to be invited in for a drink and a chat with the guards and he soon got to know all the court gossip. One time, Puss got to hear that the king was planning to drive the next day in his grand carriage with his daughter, the most beautiful princess in France. Puss took care to find out which direction they intended to take.

The next morning he said to his master, "I think it would be a good idea to take a swim in the river this morning." The lad agreed and, by the look in Puss's eye, he knew that he had a plan in mind. Puss led the way to a part of the river where the royal carriage was bound to pass. While the boy was swimming in the river, Puss heard the sound of the approaching carriage. Quickly Puss hid his master's ragged clothes under a stone and as the carriage came into view he ran into the road shouting, "Help! The Marquis of Carabas is drowning!" At once the king recognised Puss and ordered his guards to go to the rescue. The lad pretended to be drowning, so that the guards had quite a struggle to get him to the bank.

Meanwhile, Puss went up to the carriage, bowed to the king and said, "While he was bathing, thieves unfortunately stole my master's fine clothing. He cannot appear before your daughter without any clothes."

"Of course not," replied the king, and sent his footman to fetch a spare set of clothes from the back of the royal carriage. Now that the handsome lad was properly dressed, the king was glad to meet the mysterious Marquis, of whom he had heard so much from Puss. He welcomed the 'Marquis' into the carriage, where he sat next to the princess. "Come for a drive with us, my dear Marquis," said the king.

Without another word Puss set off and disappeared around the next bend of the road. By the time the king's gilded carriage was on its way again, Puss was a long way ahead. Soon he passed a field of haymakers. "My good haymakers," said Puss, "you must tell the king that this meadow belongs to the Marquis of Carabas – or I'll grind you all to little pieces."

Now Puss knew that the meadow really belonged to an ogre, who was known to be able to change his shape. So of course the haymakers had no idea if this was just an ordinary pussy cat telling them what to do – or if it really was the ogre. Soon the royal carriage passed by and the king leaned out and asked to whom the field belonged. "To the Marquis of Carabas, your majesty," chorused the haymakers.

"That's a fine piece of land you've got there," said the king, nudging the lad who was busy chatting to the princess.

All along the road it was the same story. Puss always got there before the royal carriage. Woodcutters, shepherds, and farmers all told the king that their master was the Marquis of Carabas, because Puss had threatened to turn them all into mincemeat if they didn't. Now Puss caught sight of a fine castle which he recognised as belonging to the ogre.

Puss went up to the great gate and asked to speak to the ogre. Puss said to him, "I heard that you can transform yourself in the most amazing way – into a lion for example. But I really can't believe that this is true."

The ogre was so offended that he bellowed, "JUST YOU WATCH!" and instantly turned himself into a lion. Puss pretended to be scared and jumped up on to the castle roof. The ogre turned himself back into an ogre. "That'll teach you," he roared.

"You gave me a dreadful fright," said Puss. "Do you know, people say you can even turn yourself into a tiny animal, such as rat or mouse. But that's absurd. It's quite impossible."

"IMPOSSIBLE, EH?" screeched the ogre, and the great foolish creature turned himself into a mouse.

In an instant, Puss had pounced on him and gobbled him up, bones and all. At that moment, the royal carriage rumbled over the drawbridge, for the king, too, had spotted the castle and wondered who lived there.

"Welcome to the castle of the Marquis of Carabas, your majesty," said Puss, who had just wiped the last morsels of the ogre from his whiskers.

"What," cried the king, turning to the young boy, "is this yours, too?" The lad glanced at Puss and then nodded. "May we see inside?" went on the king.

So the king, the princess and the miller's son looked around the castle. And very fine it was, too. The ogre's servants were so happy to see the back of their master that they laid on a fine feast. And at the end of the meal, the king agreed to give his daughter's hand in marriage to the 'Marquis'.

As for Puss, his master was so grateful that he saw to it that the cat was made a lord. So they all lived happily ever after and Puss never had to chase another mouse for the rest of his life.

This is a Parragon Book
This edition published in 2000

Parragon
Queen Street House
4 Queen Street
Bath BA1 1HE

Written by Derek Hall, Alison Morris and
Louisa Somerville
Illustrated by Natalie Bould, Mary Hall, Paula
Martyr, Martin Orme and Jenny Williams

Printed and bound in Spain
ISBN 0-75253-528-5